# SKY
# HUNTER

D1350470

# *ROY APPS*

Published by BBC Educational Publishing,
a division of BBC Enterprises Limited,
Woodlands, 80 Wood Lane, London W12 0TT

First published 1991
© Roy Apps/BBC Enterprises Limited 1991
The moral right of the author has been asserted.
Original story and drama
script by Leonard Kingston
Illustrations © Tracy Fennell 1991
Front and back cover illustrations © Selwyn Hutchinson
Back cover photo by C. H. Gomersall/RSPB
Cover and book design by Bernard Cavender

ISBN 0 563 34772 4

Set in Baskerville 12/15 by Ace Filmsetting Ltd, Frome, Somerset
Printed and bound in Great Britain by Clays Ltd, St Ives plc

# Contents

If you ever go to Gloucestershire and stand on top of Yat Rock, you feel like a king on the tallest turret of a mighty castle. Below is a sheer drop. At the bottom the muddy-brown River Severn, crowded with clusters of bright canoes seemingly no bigger than fishing floats, twists and loops its way between dark and thickly wooded banks. This is Symonds Yat.

With a pair of binoculars you can see the land beyond the river, where a number of narrow winding lanes carry all kinds of visitors in all kinds of vehicles towards this beauty spot: silent elderly couples in sparkling Metros, screaming school parties in battered old minibuses, tired-looking tourists peering out from behind the dusty windows of luxury coaches.

But wait! Hold your binoculars still for a moment, for there is something easing its way up the hillside track towards us that looks totally out of place.

It is a double-decker bus.

But not the usual kind of double-decker bus. No, this one has pictures of birds all over it, like a kind of giant nature painting on wheels. Its destination board doesn't read 'Piccadilly' or 'Kensington' but 'Action for Birds'. The driver—a young woman with blonde hair—slows down for a bend, changes down a gear, and then accelerates as if she has spent all her life driving her brightly-coloured bus along these narrow country lanes.

The Birdbus slows to a halt on top of Yat Rock, although the nearest bus stop must be more than five miles away. A sudden loud hiss as she applies the air brakes sends a startled bird winging its way out from the cover of the hillside.

The driver leaps out of the bus and looks up at the sky. Her two friends follow her down. One of them, a tall, black young man, points excitedly up to the sky, to where the bird they have startled is swooping in great majestic circles.

'Look, there goes the male! What a flier!' He turns to his companion. 'Hey, Butch! Do you remember the first time we saw a bird like that?' And he roars with laughter and nudges his shorter, stockier friend, who looks embarrassed.

'That was years ago! I didn't know anything about birds in those days, did I,' he says, wincing, as if from some painful memory.

The other young man stops laughing and looks thoughtful. He turns to the bus driver.

'Yes, that was a good summer, eh, Jackie?'
    'You're right, Trev. That fortnight we
spent on the old ROSIE was the best
summer holiday I ever had . . .'

# 1 Strangers on the canal

At first sight the brightly-painted narrow boat looked as if it might have been dropped into a giant vice and squeezed, it seemed so long and thin. The flat-topped cabin ran almost the whole length of the boat and on its side were painted the words 'Sharon Blake ROSIE Manchester'. Manchester was where the narrow boat came from, ROSIE was its name, and Sharon Blake was its owner. Every summer she brought the ROSIE through the canals and rivers of central England all the way down to the Regent's Canal in London.

Three heads popped up out of the deck hatch, like rabbits emerging from a burrow. The first belonged to Butch, a stocky, freckled boy. Then came his mate Trevor, tall and gangling. And last came Jackie, who was Sharon's younger cousin—which was how she and the two boys came to be spending a holiday on the ROSIE.

'We'll come back loaded!' Butch was in a buoyant mood. He waved a fishing rod in the air, menacingly. He had visions that his catch would be so big they would have trouble getting it back to the boat.

'Sez you!' said Jackie.

Trevor groaned. He knew only too well that Butch's boasting was the sort of thing that only comes from someone who has never been fishing before.

'Now listen, you just take care you don't fall into the canal and drown yourselves,' said Sharon.

'Promise,' promised Jackie.

'We *can* swim,' said Butch. 'Come on!'

As the three friends stepped off the boat and onto the towpath, Jackie turned back to her cousin. 'See you later,' she said with a knowing grin.

Sharon winked back at her. 'By the way, fish fingers for supper,' she whispered.

The voices drifted away up the towpath, until all Sharon could hear was the dull roar of an aeroplane beginning its long sweeping descent into Heathrow Airport. Sharon watched Jackie, Butch and Trevor disappear out of sight around a bend in the towpath, then she clambered back down the narrow wooden steps into the cabin. Inside, the ROSIE was a bit like the inside of a caravan. Sharon spread herself out along one of the long seats by the window that converted into a bunk. 'I don't know,' she muttered to herself. 'Those three haven't been here a week yet and they're already beginning to wear me out. What have I let myself in for?'

But, of course, she had no way of knowing that; which, given the events that were to befall the crew of the ROSIE over the next few days, was probably just as well.

Butch sighed. 'I don't reckon there are any fish in this stupid canal,' he said. 'I haven't had one bite!'

'We've only been here ten minutes,' Jackie pointed out.

Tired of watching her line bobbing up and down in the murky grey water of the canal, Jackie lay on her back and watched the clouds rolling by overhead. Suddenly her eye was drawn to the tree-tops at the edge of the cemetery on the far side of the canal.

'That's a strange bird up there. What is it?'

It was a large bird with a hooked beak and a greyish-brown mottled colour. It sat for a moment amongst the branches, proud and erect; then it swooped upwards, high above the canal.

'It's a duck,' said Butch, with all the certainty of a Mastermind finalist.

'A *duck*?' Jackie was no expert, but even she knew what a duck looked like. Her baby brother played with a plastic one in his bath every night.

'Stands to reason,' Butch retorted, 'ducks fly above water, don't they?' Trevor and Jackie groaned. 'Well, if it isn't a duck, what is it?' challenged Butch, immediately putting Trevor on the spot.

Trevor umm-ed and ah-ed. He knew he had to say something, make some sort of suggestion, just to shut Butch up. But he didn't know any more about birds than Butch. He was only familiar with pigeons and sparrows, which he often saw in London. But this bird wasn't a pigeon or a sparrow; it was far too big.

Trevor took a deep breath. 'It's an eagle,' he said, finally.

'You don't find eagles in London!' retorted Butch, scornfully.

Trevor grinned. 'Perhaps it's on holiday.'

'Hah, hah.' Butch never found Trevor's jokes very funny, particularly as he always told them when he—Butch—was trying to be serious. Jackie began to chortle, and then stopped.

'Listen!'

The strange bird was drifting, almost floating, back down to the trees. And it was making some sort of cry.

'It says kek-kek-kek, not quack-quack.'

'Definitely,' agreed Butch, using his favourite word.

The bird swooped again in a wide, graceful arc, just skimming the tops of the trees. Then it rose steeply and just hung there in the sky, its dark, wide wings beating the air, almost as in slow motion. For a minute or more, Jackie, Trevor and even Butch were silenced by this magnificent bird with no name.

'Birdie! Birdie! Birdie!'

They all looked round. Tripping along the towpath came a man and a woman. The man, overweight, sweaty and breathless, carried a large wicker basket in one hand and a lump of raw meat in the other. The woman was short and dressed in black trousers and a black leather jacket.

'Birdie! Tweet, tweet!' called the man, looking up at the sky. He and the woman in black were fast approaching Jackie, Butch and Trevor, but the man's eyes were trained skywards in search of the mysterious bird. He did not see Trevor's fishing line.

'Watch it!'

'Birdie! Bird. . . what the. . . !'

Trevor pulled desperately on his line to try and clear it of the man's legs, but the harder he pulled, the tighter the line wrapped itself around the man's ankles.

'Eeeeaoow!'

The man crashed heavily to the ground and lay at Trevor's feet, furiously trying to kick the line from his legs.

'Get up, you fool!' the woman in black yelled to her companion. Then she turned to Jackie. 'You're not allowed to fish on the towpath!' Her eyes were dark and hard. 'And you!' She turned to Trevor, who was struggling with his line as the man clambered back to his feet. 'Go away!'

Trevor looked at her for a moment, and a gleam came into his eye. 'Oh, all right,' he said, and grasping his rod firmly in both hands, he took a few paces backwards. The line pulled taut again, this time even tighter. The man staggered, desperately thrashing his arms about as if he was some kind of crazy human windmill. But to no avail. His feet slipped away from him and he fell backwards, with a satisfying splash, into the unappetising waters of the canal.

'Idiot! Don't you drop that meat!' were the woman's only words of concern. 'And get that string off your feet!'

The man stumbled out of the canal, dripping wet. His face glistened, his hair hung in rats' tails about his ears. The fall seemed to have freed him of Trevor's line. Grabbing the wicker basket, while all the time cursing and swearing at what he called 'them kids', he huffed and puffed his way along the towpath after the woman.

'You should watch where you're going,' called Jackie.

'Yes! And keep your big feet to yourself!' yelled Trevor for good measure. 'What a pair of creeps!' he muttered to himself.

The commotion seemed to have disturbed the strange bird, because when Jackie looked back to the tree-tops, they were empty and quiet, their leafy branches swaying gently in the afternoon breeze.

Butch sighed. He lay on his back with his eyes closed. Trevor nudged Jackie and grinned as he quietly bent down and gave Butch's line half a dozen sharp tugs.

'Wha-a-a? Eh?' Butch sat bolt upright and gripped his rod, determined to take the strain as he reeled in the line. 'I've caught a whopper! Gi-normous!'

Jackie spluttered, unable to stop herself. Butch shot a glance first at her, and then at Trevor, who let go of Butch's line with a tremendous chortle and rolled over and over on the grassy bank like a puppy at play.

'Very funny, Trevor!' As usual, Butch

hadn't seen the joke. He flung himself on top of Trevor, who, helpless with laughter, was unable to do much to stop him. 'Boys!' thought Jackie. 'Why do they always have to stage these pretend fights?' It was always the same, even though they were the best of mates. She sighed and glanced at her glass jar. One miserable minnow. Some catch.

'Yeowww!'

The cry came from amongst the trees in the cemetery on the other side of the canal.

'It's that man again—old big feet!'

And so it was. He was waving his right hand and swearing wildly.

'My dad does that, when he's hit his thumb with a hammer,' observed Trevor.

The children had no idea what old big feet and the woman in black were up to. But finding out looked as if it might be a more interesting way of passing the afternoon than fishing for minnows, so they ran down the towpath and over the canal bridge. There was a gap in the iron railings and they squeezed through into the cemetery.

Immediately everything seemed darker and colder. The bushes, brambles and undergrowth were lush and thick and the air had a damp feel to it. Jackie knelt down behind a grey, moss-covered gravestone which leant over at a weary angle. The boys crouched down beside her. Jackie's eye caught the rough, faded letters carved on the face of the stone: 'And also of Eliza. Rest in Peace.'

'Yeowww!' Jackie looked up and saw the man howling with pain. He was a big man and made a lot of noise. There seemed little chance of resting in peace in this graveyard. 'I give it my steak dinner and it starts eating my hand!' the man blubbered. Jackie could see that the woman was trying to bandage his hand.

'Excuse me!'

Before the boys could try to stop her, Jackie had leapt out from behind the gravestone and was approaching the strange couple.

The woman started with surprise! 'It's those kids again!' she muttered, angrily.

'My cousin Sharon's boat is only up the canal. If you come with us, she could bandage up his hand for him.'

'Kek-kek-kek.' This time another cry. The cry of the mysterious bird. Coming from the wicker basket. With the picture of the magnificent creature swooping over the tree-tops still in his mind, Trevor lifted the lid of the basket.

'Kek-kek-kek.' Far from being proud and majestic, the bird looked cowed and fearful, crouched in the bottom of the basket. It flapped and hissed and opened its curved beak out towards Trevor's hand. Suddenly the woman pushed him roughly away and slammed the lid of the basket shut.

'What kind of bird is that?' asked Trevor, with a pretend innocence.

'It's a . . . a parakeet,' the woman replied, after a moment's hesitation. She turned to the man. 'Give them some money!' she hissed.

'Money?' Butch's ears pricked up.

'We don't want your money!' said Jackie angrily, much to Butch's disappointment.

'Well go away then! Badger! Get rid of them!'

'Shoo!' said the man, as if he was trying to put the cat out. Nobody moved. 'Go on!' He lumbered along after Jackie and the boys. They could see the anger in his eyes. 'Get out!' he yelled. He meant it.

Jackie and the boys turned and ran.

Once through the fence, Trevor and Jackie turned to get a good look at old big feet. He was jammed between the railings like a nut in a pair of crackers.

But Butch ran for all he was worth towards the canal bridge. He knew, by instinct, that running was what he was good at. Other people he knew always seemed to have a clever or cheeky answer if a grown-up was yelling at them. A lot of grown-ups had yelled at Butch in their time—his dad, his older brothers, teachers at school—and he had found that his tongue was never quite sharp enough to answer them back. So he had learnt that if anyone yelled at him, the safest thing to do was *run*.

Which was why he was now on the far side of the canal bridge, struggling to get his breath back.

## 2   For sale

'Don't know why you strained yourself!' called out Trevor. 'He couldn't catch us, he was stuck!'

'I know *that*,' snapped Butch.

'Butch can't wait for his supper,' said Jackie sarcastically. She was staring at the tiny minnow, which was swimming frantically round and round the jam jar.

'If that big idiot hadn't tripped over Trevor's line, fallen in the canal and disturbed the fish, I could've caught twenty of them,' said Butch. Trevor and Jackie didn't look convinced.

'I bet we're the only people ever to go fishing for fish who ended up catching a Badger,' grinned Trevor.

'Eh?' frowned Jackie.

'What?' frowned Butch.

'That's what the woman called old big feet. Didn't you hear her? "Badger! Get rid of them!" she said to him.'

'Badger? Funny sort of name.'

'Funny sort of bloke.'

'Wait till we tell Sharon! Race you back to the boat,' yelled Butch, setting off on one of his runs.

'Hey, that's not fair!' Jackie protested. 'I've got the jam jar!'

'So?'

'So, if I run, the fish will get travel-sick!'

'Fish don't get travel-sick!' snorted Butch.

'How do you know?' replied Jackie, with a superior air. 'Have you ever asked one?'

Brightly-coloured spoons, coal-scuttles and water-cans sat drying in the evening sun all along the roof of the ROSIE. Sharon had spent the afternoon painting them with curly patterns and designs.

'About time too,' she said, as Jackie and the boys approached. 'I've got to get this lot up to the craft shop.' She stared at the minnow in the jam jar. 'And where's the rest of the fish? Too many to carry?' She laughed.

'Sorry, Sharon, only we . . .'

For a moment, Jackie didn't quite know where to start. But as the afternoon's events flashed through her mind, one picture kept coming back more vividly than the others. A picture of the greyish-brown bird, winging, swooping, diving through the pale blue sky.

'First we saw a parakeet, but I don't think it was a parakeet. Then we met this man and this woman who told us it *was* a parakeet, but Butch says it was a duck, but it went kek-kek-kek and not quack-quack, and what does a parakeet look like?'

Sharon frowned. 'A bit like a parrot, I think. I'll look it up in my bird book.'

Sharon's bird book had pictures of all the birds of the world. They studied the picture of a parakeet. It was bright green.

Trevor shook his head. 'The bird we saw was sort of greyish-brown.'

'But its beak was hooked like a parakeet's. It might've been a rare kind of dark-brown parakeet!' Butch sounded excited. 'Definitely!'

Jackie and Trevor both looked at him and sighed.

'I only said it *might've* been,' muttered Butch.


The ROSIE chugged its way down the canal towards the craft shop. Trevor sat on the deck and half-closed his eyes, so that the tall flats beyond the towpath were blocked out. Instead he concentrated his eyes on the trees and flowers at the canal's edge. That way he could almost imagine they were in the country, and not in the middle of London.

As Sharon steered the ROSIE into the narrow canal lock, Jackie felt a sudden pang of fear. The boat seemed to be trapped. And the lock seemed like a tiny, dark prison. Her mind turned once again to the strange bird that wasn't a parakeet. Only this time, she saw it trapped and frightened in the basket.

The boys were quick to undo the top lock gate, though, and the water rushed in noisily. Slowly the ROSIE began to rise, and everything cheered up as the sky grew bigger and brighter once more.

Rows of terraced houses ran along this part of the canal. Some of them had little gates leading from the garden straight onto the towpath.

'It'd be great to live in one of those, eh, Sharon?' sighed Butch.

'Those two don't seem too happy about it,' laughed Sharon. In one of the gardens two people were arguing loudly.

'Sharon! Slow down! It's them!' Jackie could hardly control her excitement.

There was no doubt about it. It was Badger and the woman in black. Their voices carried quite clearly across the canal bank . . .

'. . . I've been doing my best. I've tried everywhere. Honest!' That was Badger.

'. . . Don't give me any more excuses. You're nothing but a cheap small-time crook, and the sooner I get rid of you, the better!' That was the woman in black.

The woman marched into the house, and Badger sat all forlorn on an upturned rubber dinghy. Butch felt almost sorry for him. He well knew the feeling of always being blamed for everything. Suddenly Badger turned towards the ROSIE. Jackie, Trevor and Butch ducked out of sight into the cabin.

'What do you think of that?' whispered Jackie excitedly. ' "Crook" she called him!'

Sharon shrugged. 'People say that without really meaning it.'

Trevor shook his head. 'You could tell! She meant it all right.'

24

Jackie was jumping up and down. 'Can we stop? We might hear something else!'

'Look, Jackie, I've got to get these water-cans to the craft centre. I haven't got time to play detectives.'

'But . . .' Jackie caught Sharon's eye and could tell. She meant it.

After the water-cans had been delivered to the craft shop, Sharon said, 'Right! Supper. We'd best *fry* that minnow you caught. Jackie can have the tail, Trevor the middle and Butch the head.'

'What?' Butch's face was very troubled.

Sharon laughed. 'Don't look so worried, Butch! There's only one place for that minnow—and it's not in my frying pan. No, you'd best tip it back into the canal.'

'But what about supper?' Butch's face was still troubled.

'I know a place where we can all catch some decent fish for supper.'

'Where's that?'

'At the bottom of my freezer bag.'

'Eh?'

'Go on, put your hand in.'

Butch thrust his hand into the freezer bag and pulled out a large packet of fish fingers.

25

That night Jackie lay in her bunk and felt the gentle movement of the ROSIE as it bobbed up and down on the silent canal. She turned and stretched and tried counting backwards from a hundred, but she still couldn't get to sleep. She couldn't stop thinking about the mysterious bird they had seen swooping in such broad circles in the late afternoon sky. The same bird that Badger and the woman in black were keeping trapped in the wicker basket. Why?

'Why?' Jackie asked after lunch. 'Why should they *want* the bird? I mean, what could they do with it?'

Butch, of course, knew the answer.

'They're breeding 'em. Masses of special parakeets.'

'If it *is* a parakeet.'

'All right, masses of whatever it is. Then one day they'll let them attack a . . . a train, say! A train carrying bank notes!' Trevor and Jackie stared at Butch in open-mouthed wonder. Where did he get his ideas from? Butch caught their stares, and assumed them to be the looks of two people awestruck by his incredible intelligence. He went on, acting out the scenario with his hands. 'And the birds would fly straight at the driver, see . . . Neeowwwww! And then they would have to stop the train and give up all the money.'

Trevor coughed, politely. 'And would the birds be trained to carry off the notes in their beaks?'

Butch knitted his brows in serious consideration of Trevor's question. 'Mmmmm . . . Well . . . Maybe.'

'Or perhaps they'd have little money-boxes tied to their legs.'

'I don't think—'

Trevor and Jackie spluttered with laughter, and even Sharon grinned. Butch grabbed Trevor by the collar and then Trevor tried to twist Butch's arm behind his back. They were at it again.

'Hey! Stop that, you two! This is a canal boat, not a wrestling ring!'

'Well . . .' muttered Butch.

'Well . . .' muttered Trevor.

'Well . . . I've got some work to do,' said Sharon firmly. 'Jackie, I thought you were planning to visit Mr Trim again?'


Mr Trim's antique shop was one of Jackie's favourite places. As you pushed open the door, a real bell tinkled above your head. The shop itself was full of old dark chairs and cabinets. Clocks hung on the wall, each of them ticking away a different time. But the best thing about Mr Trim's shop was that you could buy little old things really cheaply. Last summer Jackie had bought a necklace of different shaped black beads for 50p. She kept it in her bedside drawer at home and only wore it on special occasions, like parties and school discos. She had taken the boys to Mr Trim's the very first day they had arrived on the ROSIE. Butch had his eye on a second-hand camera.

'Aaaargh!'

Jackie's thoughts were stopped by a cry from Butch. He stood on the pavement clutching his stomach. Jackie recognised his symptoms immediately. 'Oh no, Butch. Not more sweets.'

Butch shook his head. 'Chocolate!' he gasped. 'I must have chocolate.' Jackie sighed in despair. Once, after Butch had stayed for tea, her mum had said, 'I hope you don't bring him home for tea too often, love. He's got through a whole pot of jam. I think he's got hollow legs.'

Butch dived into a nearby newsagent's, and Jackie and Trevor hung around outside. The newsagent's was full of cards advertising second-hand cars, lost cats and old furniture. Jackie's eye was caught by one card in particular. 'Hey! Look at this!' She pointed the card out to Trevor.

```
┌─────────────────────────────────────────┐
│                                         │
│              FOR SALE                   │
│        Small chest of drawers           │
│                                         │
│           with  contents                │
│                                         │
│         e.g.  rare specimens            │
│              £ 500                       │
│                        Charles J. Trim  │
│        Inspection      (Antiques) Ltd   │
│         invited        26 Cheap Street  │
│                                         │
└─────────────────────────────────────────┘
```

'Five hundred quid!' Trevor whistled. 'For a chest of drawers! I don't believe it!'

Butch joined them, his mouth full of chocolate. 'It shubb—'

'Butch.'

'Wobb?'

'Don't try and speak when you've got a mouth full of chocolate.'

'With contents?' Trevor shot Jackie a puzzled look.

Butch swallowed his last chunk of chocolate.

'That's what I was saying. You don't

usually sell furniture with things in it, do you?'

Trevor shrugged. 'Mr Trim obviously does.'

Butch looked at the card again. 'And what does e.g. mean?'

Trevor grinned, broadly. He could feel another joke coming on. 'E.g. spells egg. The contents must be eggs.'

'Eh?' said Butch.

This time even Jackie missed the joke. 'Don't be silly! E.g. means "for example".'

But Trevor's grin got broader still. 'That's what I said! Eggs-ample! Get it!' Jackie groaned and rolled her eyes. Butch still looked puzzled.

'Eggs?' Trevor and the other two spun round to find themselves facing an angry face. A youngish man, tall, with a thick moustache and keen eyes. Jackie and Butch took a couple of paces back.

'Did you say *eggs*? What kind of eggs?' The man was insistent.

Trevor shuffled uneasily. 'Er . . . I was only joking . . .' He waved a hand half-heartedly at the shop window. The man spotted the card, read it intently, then spun round to face Trevor again.

'Joking?' His tone was fierce, unrelenting.

He looked right down into Trevor's eyes. 'What is this? Do you kids know anything about this card? Do you know this Mr Trim?'

'Er . . . yes,' said Jackie, quietly.

'Not really,' said Trevor.

'Er, no, definitely not!' added Butch. He had that familiar and sickening feeling that he was about to get blamed again for something he hadn't done. But the man had already turned and walked into the newsagent's.

'Let's scarper,' whispered Trevor, who had also sensed trouble.

The three of them sprinted off up the street. At the corner Jackie glanced round. Just in time to see the angry young man close the newsagent's door behind him and break into a run. In their direction.

'Come on!' she yelled. 'He's after us!'

# 3 The Birdman

The shop bell rang with its familiar dull tinkle. Trevor's sharp eyes scoured the street as he closed the door, but there was no sign of the angry young man.

'Ah! My little sailor friends! Greetings!' Mr Trim beamed at them. Butch, who had spent many a day running away from park keepers and school caretakers, went immediately to position himself by the window. But Trevor and Jackie just stood there, still panting from their run, trying to get their breath back.

'Hello . . . Mr . . . Trim . . .'

'My dears, you do seem to be in a hurry!'

If she was honest with herself, Jackie never really liked the way Mr Trim called them his 'dears' and his '*little* sailor friends'. She felt that at any moment he was going to pat her gently on the head, the way you do babies in pushchairs. But she put it down to the fact that he was old. Indeed Mr Trim seemed to be more ancient and wrinkled each time they saw him. His white hair hung in a shaggy mane over his ears. Jackie noticed that his jacket seemed to sag about his shoulders and that his bow tie, instead of being dead horizontal at a quarter to three, had drooped at both ends to twenty to four.

Trevor was more interested in the contents of the shop than he was in Mr Trim. He ran his finger along the top of the glass case, leaving a long, clear furrow in the dust. £10 said a little white sticker. A table stood next to it. It was scratched and one leg stuck out at an odd angle—£5. What was Mr Trim doing with a chest of drawers worth £500?

'Short of cash are we?'

Trevor turned his head and saw Jackie nodding. Was she going to say anything about the chest of drawers? Mr Trim was her friend rather than his and Butch's, after all.

But Mr Trim went on. 'Never mind. We're sure to find something cheap.' He shuffled across the shop and lifted down a large black tray from the top of a cabinet. The sight of it immediately made Butch leave his guard post by the window.

'Have you still got that camera, Mr Trim?' he asked eagerly.

'I think I may have. Have a look . . .'

The tray was a treasure trove. You never knew quite what you might find. Trevor picked up a magnifying glass and an old medal and tried them out, eager to find

something that worked, that would impress people at school. Jackie, though, couldn't help wondering where all these objects had come from. What kind of letters had been written with the funny pen with the spiky nib? Who was the sad-looking sailor in the tiny black-and-white photograph? Did he go to war on his ship? Did he come back? Meanwhile Butch had found the camera and was looking at things all round the room. He watched the pendulum on a wall clock swing to and fro. He watched Mr Trim's face.

He watched the shop door swing open.

The angry young man stood there, and a hard look came into his eye as he saw Butch.

The tinkle of the door bell caused Jackie and Trevor to look up. Then they looked down again at the tray and busied themselves with knick-knacks, as if this might somehow make them invisible. A shiver ran down Jackie's spine.

'Do come in, sir,' Mr Trim was saying. 'My, my, the shop *is* full of customers all of a sudden! How can I help you, sir?'

'Just looking around.' The young man was gruff and terse.

A kind of expectant excitement hung in the air. Even the clocks seemed to be ticking faster. The stranger moved from one piece of furniture to another. Floorboards creaked with every step. Jackie looked at the photograph of the sailor, but her interest in him was gone. Trevor studied his medal through unseeing eyes. Butch fingered the camera, nervously.

'Not damaged, I hope?' Mr Trim's voice came out shrill and loud.

'No. It's all right. Definitely!' Butch could hear everyone listening. 'How much is it?'

'To you, Butch, fifty pence.'

'Thanks, Mr Trim . . .'

But Mr Trim had lost interest in Butch and was looking past him. Butch turned to see the stranger crouching down by a small chest of drawers in the darkest corner of the shop. He pulled at the top drawer, roughly; but it seemed to be stuck.

'Just a moment, do you mind, sir?' Mr Trim had become suddenly curt.

'How much is this chest of drawers?'

Jackie was surprised to see how quickly Mr Trim moved to place himself between the stranger and the chest of drawers.

'That chest is already sold.'

'For five hundred pounds?'

A strange sort of smile curled round Mr Trim's lips.

The stranger grew angry. 'The drawers appear to be stuck.'

'That may be because they *are* stuck.' But Mr Trim's attempted joke fell heavily in the highly-charged atmosphere. 'I'm afraid you'll have to wait, sir. I'm attending to other customers.' He was still smiling as he walked over to Jackie and Trevor, but the stranger followed.

'I just wondered what exactly are the *contents* of the drawers?' He paused, pulled a picture from his pocket and then flashed it

menacingly in Mr Trim's face. 'Have they got anything to do with this?'

Jackie got only a glimpse of the picture, but there was no mistaking the greyish-brown plumage, the hooked beak. 'That's our bird!' she cried, before she had time to realise what she was saying.

The stranger rounded on her.

'Your bird? What do you mean, *your* bird?' he barked.

'I don't mean it's ours . . . I mean . . . We saw a bird like that . . .' Why was she saying this, to this stranger? Jackie felt flustered.

'Where? Where?' the stranger was close to

her now, too close, glaring intently.

'I . . . I . . .'

'Just a moment, sir!' Suddenly Mr Trim stepped forward and pushed the young man away from Jackie. He staggered backwards, knocking a tall vase onto the floor with a crash. 'You leave these children alone!' Mr Trim's voice quivered with rage. 'They are friends of mine and I will not have them bullied by any brash young man who pushes his way into my shop. Out! Out of my shop. Or there will be trouble!'

Surprised by the spirit and force of the old man's words, the stranger backed out through the door.

Mr Trim turned the lock and pulled down the blind.

'Are you all right, Mr Trim?' asked Jackie, still afraid the stranger would start hammering on the window.

'Yes, yes, my dear. Now tell me everything you know about the bird.'

'It's a parakeet . . .' began Butch.

Mr Trim held up his hand. 'Parakeet! My dear young friends, that was no parakeet. Don't you realise that was a picture of a peregrine falcon? What you saw was a falcon!'

'A peregrine falcon?'

'Yes! One of the rarest wild birds in Britain.'

'It wasn't wild when we last saw it,' thought Jackie, recalling the frightened eyes staring up at them from the bottom of the wicker basket.

'Now, my dears.' Mr Trim was almost back to his usual grandfatherly self. 'Just tell me everything. From the beginning.'

The fishing trip . . . the basket . . . the woman in black . . . the house by the canal . . . between them the story all came out. Mr Trim nodded, frowned, shook his head, frowned again.

After they had finished, they waited for Mr Trim to say something, anything. But he just sat heavily in his old leather chair, his pale eyes brooding. The clocks ticked expectantly in the background.

'Mr Trim . . . ?'

'Mmmmm?'

'What does it all mean?'

'It means, my dears—unless I am very much mistaken—that poor beautiful peregrine falcon has been stolen. Perhaps from its nest in the mountains of Scotland. The thieves must have brought it down to

London to sell.' He shook his head, sadly. 'Peregrine falcons can fly faster than any other bird in Britain. People all over the world pay a lot of money for such a rare bird.' He paused, and added quietly, almost as an afterthought, 'Or its eggs.'

Trevor looked puzzled. 'What's wrong with that?'

Butch raised his eyebrows. 'It's against the law?' he asked Mr Trim, more as a matter of fact than a question.

'Indeed it is! It's stealing to take a falcon or its eggs from a nest. Why, if these things are allowed to go on, they say that very soon there'll be no wild falcons left in Britain!'

Jackie was filled with a sudden anger. 'And that . . . that creepy man who was in here was obviously after *our* falcon!' It didn't bear thinking about.

Mr Trim nodded. There was a strange, sad look in his eyes, as if he too found it painful to think that people were driven by greed or desperation to do such things. 'It was very lucky I was here to deal with him, my dears. You see, I am an ELF.'

Trevor sniggered. 'You're a bit big for an elf, Mr Trim!'

'I was a pixie once, in the Brownies,' said Jackie. 'But that,' she added pointedly, 'was a very long time ago.'

Mr Trim smiled. 'ELF stands for the English Lovers of the Falcon. E.L.F.'

'Oh yes, of course,' nodded Butch.

'We ELFs are sworn to try to save and protect our wild falcons!'

'What do you want us to do, Mr Trim?' asked Trevor enthusiastically.

'Come down the canal with me and show me which house you saw that man and woman come out of.'

'Do you reckon they're falcon thieves as well?' Jackie was trying to fit the pieces of the jigsaw together. 'Do you reckon they're in it with the man who came in here?'

Mr Trim nodded. 'Yes, them and the Birdman.'

'This'll scare them!' Trevor took a dusty-looking sword down from a shelf. He tried to wave it in the air, but it was too heavy.

'No, no, my dears! We are going to spy out the land, as it were,' said Mr Trim, nervously.

'Definitely,' agreed Butch.

Mr Trim picked up a battered walking stick, and Jackie, Trevor and Butch followed him to the door. It was while Mr Trim was bending down to lock up the shop that Jackie saw the flash of a face as it shot down behind the cover of a parked van.

'It's him! It's the Birdman!'

'Back inside, my dears, quickly!'

Jackie had half a mind to chase after the Birdman, but in no time at all Mr Trim had ushered them all back inside the shop.

'We could fight him,' said Butch.

'Yes, there's three of us—four with you, Mr Trim!' added Trevor, excitedly.

'No . . . no . . .' Mr Trim sounded agitated. 'I don't want him following us . . .'

'If he does, we'll call the police!'

'No! No!'

'Why not?'

Mr Trim did not seem to hear Jackie's question. He seemed to be thinking aloud. 'The back door, yes, that's it . . . the back door! Come on . . .'

They slipped out through the back of the shop. On their way they passed the £500 chest of drawers.

'Mr Trim! What *is* in those . . . ?' asked Trevor. But his question drifted into empty air, for Mr Trim and the other two were already out of the building and in the back yard.

'Come along!' called Mr Trim. 'We mustn't let that Birdman follow us! We musn't let him meet the other two!'

A dull tinkling was heard as the door of the unlocked shop was opened. The determined face of the Birdman broke into a quiet smile as his eyes lighted once again on the £500 chest of drawers.

## 4 Too many crooks!

'That's the house where we saw them. Definitely!' yelled Butch as he, Jackie and Trevor raced along the towpath.

Old Mr Trim stumbled along behind, prodding the ground with his walking stick. Trevor observed the fence that stood between them and the garden of the house.

'It's all broken down—let's go in and storm the house!'

'No, no,' Mr Trim gasped, and leant heavily on his stick, trying to get his breath back. 'First we must wait and watch, my dears. You know, spy out the land.'

Trevor could scarcely control his frustration. Spy out the land? They had the woman in black and Badger cornered. Through the fence he could see a wooden shed. He turned imploringly to Mr Trim.

'But Mr Trim! I bet the bird's in that shed!'

Suddenly Jackie let out a desperate whisper. 'Trevor! Butch! Mr Trim! Down!'

Down went their heads, like ducks in a shooting gallery. They could see the heavy form of Badger emerging from the house. In his hand was a white tin plate, the sort you

use when camping. On the plate was a large
red lump of raw meat. Badger studied the
lump of meat, almost fondly, then he
lumbered down the untidy garden to the
shed and in one clumsy movement
unlatched the door, tossed the meat in and
slammed the door shut. He glanced furtively
round about him, then stumbled through
the bushes back to the house.

'You see! The bird *is* there!' Trevor had
already climbed over the broken fence
palings.

'Definitely!' Butch was clambering after
him.

'Hurry up, you two!' Jackie shoved them
from behind.

'Er . . . yes. I think we might now venture in and have a look. Er . . . quietly, my dears,' mumbled Mr Trim, with some agitation.

The shed door creaked on its hinges.

The narrow shaft of dusty sunlight showed them all they needed to see.

'Kek-kek-kek.'

The bird's frightened eyes stared out at them, unblinkingly. Jackie was the first to see that it was tied to a post.

'Is it a peregrine falcon, Mr Trim?' was all she could manage to say.

Mr Trim seemed to be staring straight down into the magnificent bird's eyes. He nodded, distantly, as if somehow his mind was somewhere else.

'We were right, then?' insisted Trevor, determined to make his point.

'Oh yes, my dears. So right. This is the peregrine falcon.'

'Kek-kek-kek.'

The falcon's strong talons and hooked beak tore angrily at the raw meat.

'So beautiful . . .' whispered Mr Trim.

'Beautiful,' echoed Jackie. Then suddenly her sense of awe turned to anger. 'No wild

bird should be tied up like that!'

For a moment, Mr Trim seemed genuinely taken aback by the passion in her eyes.

'Shall we tell the fuzz?' Already Trevor was imagining a massive stake out, with helicopters, dogs, marksmen, police launches on the canal . . . Trevor watched a lot of television.

Mr Trim looked startled. 'No . . . no.' He looked from Trevor to Jackie to Butch, then pulled himself up to his full height and announced with the finality of someone who has made up his mind once and for all, 'I'm going into the house to talk to them.'

'Mr Trim!' Jackie could not hide the fear in her voice.

'But . . .' Trevor wanted to say 'but you're a weak old man' but he didn't think it would sound too good, so he mumbled, 'they might murder you!' Then wished he hadn't.

'We'll come with you,' said Butch, and he meant it.

'Oh, Butch, thank you. But no, I want you all to stay here, out of sight. If I'm not out in, say, five minutes, well then you can go for the fuzz, er . . . police.'

With an air of self-importance, Butch checked his watch. 'Right, I'll keep the time.'

'Do watch out, Mr Trim,' implored Jackie.

'I will, my dear. Don't worry.'

Jackie, Trevor and Butch crawled back behind the fence and, crouching low, watched Mr Trim's frail figure totter up the garden towards the house. The house looked totally dilapidated. The brickwork was discoloured with bright green marks where rain water had poured from the rusty drainpipes. Next to the back door was a small outhouse—an old-fashioned outside toilet—with a bright blue door swinging on one rusty hinge. The back door to the house itself was covered in blotches and peeling dark green paint. Mr Trim rapped firmly on the door with his stick.

'If they dare jump him . . .' muttered Butch.

'Sssh!' hissed Jackie and Trevor together.

The back door of the house edged open. Then it swung fully open and Badger stood on the doorstep, towering over Mr Trim and staring down into his face with a startled look.

'What do you think he's saying?' asked Jackie, uneasily.

'How should I know? They're too far away to hear,' Trevor snapped back.

So they just watched, while Butch checked his watch once more.

'Right, Badger, you worm. We meet again.'

'Trim!'

'Quiet you fool! *Smile*! We're being watched. Smile I said! And ask me to come in.'

This is the conversation that Jackie, Trevor and Butch would have heard, had they been on the doorstep with Badger and Mr Trim. But all they could hear from their hiding place on the far side of the fence was a low drone of traffic somewhere in the background and the shrill chorus of excited sparrows and starlings high above them.

What they *saw* was Badger opening his arms and ushering their friend, the frail and elderly Mr Trim, into the house.

'Five minutes,' muttered Butch. 'Just five minutes.'


The door closed on Mr Trim and Badger.

'Four minutes forty-five seconds . . .' intoned Butch.

'Just shut up!' said Trevor, annoyed that Butch, and not he, was the one with the watch.

Butch gave Trevor a shove.

Jackie couldn't believe it. They were at it again. 'Stop arguing, you two! This is serious!' She half-expected to hear cries for help coming from the house. She just hoped that her old friend Mr Trim was all right.


Jackie could not have known this, but her old friend Mr Trim was in fact doing very nicely, thank you.

'What are you trying to keep me out of?

Who's in this with you?' he hissed, angrily.

Badger stumbled back against the wall, caught off-guard by the old gentleman's sudden show of strength. In a flash, Mr Trim's hands were round his walking stick and the walking stick was rammed hard against Badger's throat. Badger's cheeks flushed bright red and a kind of strangled gurgling sound spluttered from his lips. Mr Trim eased the pressure just a fraction.

'MacBride . . .' gasped Badger. 'She's the one . . .'

'You want to talk to me?' Instinctively Mr Trim increased the pressure on Badger's throat before turning round. What he saw, leaning against the doorpost with an unconcerned air, her arms folded across her chest, was the sinister figure of the woman in black.

'*The* Miss MacBride? The one they call "Cat Mary"?'

The woman in black shrugged. 'Some call me that.'

'The great falcon thief.' Mr Trim's tone was admiring.

A brief smirk passed across Cat Mary's stony face.

'Trim, you're . . . you're choking me!' spluttered a voice behind Mr Trim.

'Be quiet, you great bag of lard.'

He had forgotten Badger, and even now as he finally removed his stick from old big feet's neck, he did it as if his mind was on more important things. Badger slumped down onto a chair.

'Trim is it?' Cat Mary stayed in the doorway.

Mr Trim nodded.

'What's your game?'

As Mr Trim advanced on Cat Mary, she put out a warning hand. Mr Trim smiled his best Antique Shop owner's smile. 'I buy and I sell, Miss MacBride. In the rare-bird trade, you understand.' His old eyes twinkled in the dim light. 'I'm surprised Badger here hasn't arranged to put you in touch with me.'

'Him? He couldn't arrange a bunch of daffodils!'

Badger tried to speak but could only manage a red-faced wheeze.

'He promised me he could sell that falcon out there in the shed,' Cat Mary went on, 'that valuable rare bird that I'd gone all the way to the Scottish Highlands to acquire—'

'Nick, you mean,' muttered Badger, who had finally found his voice again.

Mr Trim's smile broadened. 'Miss MacBride,' he said with an air of finality, 'your luck has changed. I can sell the bird for you. I'm smuggling some falcons' eggs to a French buyer tonight. He's on a boat on the river this very moment. He'll pay big money for that bird.'

'How big?'

'Two thousand.'

Cat Mary's eyes gleamed.

'But I'll take half as my cut.' Now it was the turn of Mr Trim's eyes to gleam.

Cat Mary's eyes immediately darkened.

'You won't.'

'Miss MacBride . . .' Mr Trim sounded so helpful, so reasonable. 'I have three young kids waiting outside, all about to run and call the police.'

'Police?' Badger's reflexes had conditioned him to twitch at the sound of the word.

'You know, Badger,' Mr Trim put on his bedtime-story-voice, 'men in white cars with bright blue flashing lights on the top.'

Cat Mary was already peering behind the tattered curtain and shaking her head. Badger stared out over her shoulder. 'Oh no. Them again!'

'Friends of yours, Badger?' grinned Mr Trim, knowingly. He took a pocket watch from his waistcoat. 'Well, Miss MacBride, you have one minute to make up your mind.'


'One minute,' whispered Butch breathlessly, his eyes firmly on his watch. 'Time's almost up.'

'I've never made a 999 call before,' said Trevor excitedly.

Jackie said nothing. Her eyes and her thoughts were firmly on the house and what might be going on in there.

'Well, what do you say?' asked Mr Trim, with the certainty of a man who knows exactly what the answer will be before the question has been asked.

'You win,' muttered Cat Mary, grudgingly.

'You're very wise,' smiled Mr Trim, sweetly. He put his hand on the door handle, but Cat Mary suddenly pulled him back with a look of alarm.

'We need them in here.' Mr Trim was in control. 'Now, smile. Smile everybody . . .'

Badger groaned. 'How can I? Them little brats—'

'Smile!'

Badger pulled his lips apart, so that his expression was one of an overgrown baby with a bad bout of wind. Cat Mary tried to smile too, but her nose curled up, as if she had just detected a nasty odour.

'Now keep smiling!' Yes, Mr Trim was in control.

'Forty. Thirty-nine, thirty-eight . . .'

Butch was well into his countdown when Jackie suddenly said, 'The door's opening!'

Mr Trim appeared, smiling, beckoning. Behind stood Cat Mary, smiling; and Badger, smiling.

Butch had stopped counting. Trevor frowned and Jackie's jaw dropped a mile. Nothing seemed to make sense any more.

Suddenly Mr Trim's eye was caught by something happening along the towpath on the far side of the canal. The look on his face turned to one of frenzied panic. He ushered Cat Mary and Badger inside and slammed the door shut.

Instinctively Jackie, Butch and Trevor turned round.

A little way up the towpath on the opposite side of the canal they saw the familiar figure of the Birdman. He was standing, as still and as silent as a statue, beside a large oak tree, quite oblivious that Jackie and the boys were watching him. His concentration was centred elsewhere, for he was holding a pair of powerful binoculars to his eyes.

And he had then firmly trained on the back door of the house.

## 5 The Welsh telegram

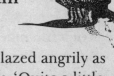

'My, my!' Cat Mary's eyes blazed angrily as she turned from the window. 'Quite a little party you've brought with you, Trim.'

Any remaining colour had now drained from Mr Trim's cheeks. Badger said nothing but stood peering anxiously through the dirty window at the Birdman.

'Who is that man?' Cat Mary's tone was as icy as ever.

Mr Trim shrugged. 'I'm not sure. But he knows something.'

Badger's attention had turned to the shuffling figures of Jackie, Trevor and Butch. He began muttering dark threats about what he would like to do to them, if only he could get his hands round their throats.

'I want them in here.' Mr Trim was beginning to recover some of his old poise.

'What! I'm not opening that door again!' Like a lot of big men with loud voices, Badger panicked easily.

Cat Mary looked sceptical.

'You want to sell the bird, don't you? You want your money?'

There was, of course, only one answer to

that question, and Cat Mary did not bother to reply.

'Then trust me!' The antique dealer's sweetest smile returned to his face. 'Watch this.'

'. . . Three, two, one!' Butch looked up from his watch. 'That's it! The five minutes is up.'

Jackie and the boys had dodged round the side of the shed to avoid being spotted by the Birdman.

'Let's rush the house!' As always, Trevor was eager for some action. 'They've obviously got him. Poor old geezer.'

'Definitely,' agreed Butch. 'But what about the Birdman? He might see us.'

Jackie looked round the side of the shed and her head shot suddenly back.

'The door's opening again!'

All three of them peered round the corner of the shed and saw, to their surprise, the figure of Mr Trim in the half-open doorway.

'All's well, my dears!' he called. 'But come quickly! Quickly and quietly!'

Keeping their heads well down, Jackie, Trevor and Butch ran up the garden, through the half-open door and into the back kitchen.

As quick as a flash, Mr Trim locked it behind them.

Jackie was looking hard at her friend old Mr Trim, still anxious in case he had been hurt in some way. Mr Trim's eyes, like those of Butch and Trevor, were drawn to the far side of the kitchen. There stood Badger and Cat Mary, awkward and uncomfortable. Jackie caught Cat Mary's eye, but she looked away, unable to face her. Trevor and Butch had their sights fixed on Badger, whose eyes twitched nervously as he attempted, unsuccessfully, to smile.

'Now, now, my dears, nothing to fear.' Mr Trim's soothing tones seemed to be applied as equally to Cat Mary and Badger as to Butch, Trevor and Jackie.

A feeling of acute unease crept over Jackie. She looked around at the filthy peeling wallpaper, the patches of damp, the single, dripping tap and the empty beer bottles.

'Lovely kids!' said Badger suddenly to Mr Trim, and he worked his mouth open into a smile. Even Cat Mary seemed taken aback.

Mr Trim covered up the ensuing silence. 'And very intelligent,' he added, with his eyes fixed firmly on Cat Mary's.

'Oh yeah! I thought that from our very first meeting!' Badger paused. 'Ha! Ha!' he added. Neither his words nor his laugh sounded at all right. It was as if they were coming from a robot. Trevor was reminded of English lessons at school, with somebody reading aloud from a book very slowly and very nervously.

Jackie appealed to her old friend. 'Mr Trim . . . What does this all mean?'

Mr Trim stood behind the three friends and put his arms round their shoulders in a fatherly fashion. 'I'll tell you, my dears. But first, let me introduce you. These people are very old friends of mine—meet Mr, er . . .'

'Badger,' said Badger.

'Er, yes . . . Mr Badger,' repeated Mr Trim, 'and Miss MacBride.'

Cat Mary tried to smile, but it still came out as a glower. 'How do you do, children?' she asked, awkwardly.

Butch's mind was a whirl. He knew that the real name of the fat man wriggling and twitching on the far side of the kitchen was no more 'Mr Badger' than his was 'Mr Butch'.

'They found the peregrine. They thought it must be stolen. They were trying to save it,' Mr Trim was explaining.

Badger nodded furiously, Cat Mary glowered, but Mr Trim's smile remained steady.

'You see, Miss MacBride is a great bird-lover.'

'So why did they tell us it was a parakeet?' asked Jackie, doubtfully.

It was a good question, but Mr Trim had the answer. 'In case you met the real thief and accidentally spilt the beans, as they say!'

'Ah yes! That's why!' Badger agreed with relief.

His voice was beginning to irritate Trevor. 'Where did the peregrine come from in the first place, then?'

Badger's jaw dropped. 'Er . . .'

It was another good question, but Mr Trim was equal to it and had the answer. He jerked a thumb towards the window.

'You mean the Birdman!' At last Jackie could see the meaning of it all.

Mr Trim nodded. 'We think he must have stolen it from its nest and brought it to London. But he lost it. Now he's trying to get it back, of course!'

'Of course . . .' Jackie nodded eagerly, relieved by her old friend's explanation.

'Definitely,' agreed Butch.

'We must send a message for help to another ELF—a friend of mine from the English Lovers of the Falcon.' Mr Trim hastily wrote a note on a scrap of paper, folded it up and handed it to Jackie. 'Take this telegram to the Post Office, my dears. We must stay here and guard the falcon. Here's some money—you can keep the change.'

Mr Trim hurried Jackie, Butch and Trevor out into the hallway.

'You must use the front door. The back's too dangerous, with the Birdman watching.'

Trevor had taken the telegram from Jackie and was studying it. 'What kind of message is this? I don't understand a word of it.'

But, again, Mr Trim had the answer. 'Ah, that's because I had to write it in Welsh. My friend is Welsh, you see. It just says that we have found a stolen wild falcon. I've told him to bring help. Now run along, my little sailor friends!'

Jackie, Trevor and Butch sprinted off down the road towards the shops.


'Welsh?' Cat Mary barked at Mr Trim as soon as he had shut the door on the young messengers.

'Of course it's not Welsh!' he snapped back. 'But if they believe it's Welsh, they won't find it a strange message.'

'But what if they . . .'

Mr Trim stared Cat Mary in the face. 'Listen! Forget about them! I've got them completely under my thumb.'

Yes, Mr Trim had the answer to everything.

Or had he?


Jackie ran panting into the tiny Post Office, Butch and Trevor close on her heels.

'Get a telegram form, Butch.'

'Right.' Sometimes Jackie just seemed

naturally to be in charge, and this was one of those times.

Trevor frowned over the telegram message. 'Look at that! Glad I'm not Welsh.'

The three of them tried pronouncing the Welsh words.

'Dedda ot sgge . . .'

'Careful, Butch!'

It was difficult to say any of them without getting spit everywhere. Jackie began copying out Mr Trim's message on the telegram form.

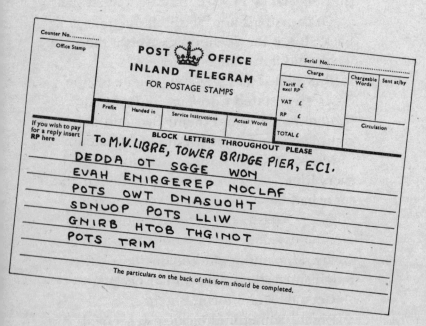

'I don't understand it.' There was a trace of anxiety in Jackie's voice.

'Of course you don't. It's Welsh!' Trevor laughed, and even Butch got the joke this time. But Jackie's face clouded with anger.

'I don't mean that, stupid. I mean I don't understand why there aren't any "stop" words.'

' "Stop" words?' Now it was Butch's turn not to understand.

'You know. In telegrams you always have to write "stop" where you would put a full stop, so that people will be able to read the message properly.'

'Well, Mr Trim would've written "stop" in Welsh, wouldn't he?'

They joined the straggling queue for the Post Office counter. In front of them and behind, old ladies in woolly hats and old gentlemen in checked caps waited patiently with their pension books. Trevor and Butch spent the waiting time playing an imaginary game of football, but Jackie continued to study the Welsh telegram. When their turn eventually came, the clerk took one look at the message and said, 'What's this?'

'Welsh,' replied Jackie, in a very matter-of-fact way.

'Welsh? That isn't Welsh!'

'How do you know?' Butch's tone was almost threatening. The Post Office clerk glowered at him.

'Because, young man, I am Welsh myself. If that's Welsh, then I'm a Dutchman. Well, are you sending this telegram or not?'

'Sorry.' Jackie realised she was still clutching Mr Trim's money.

Butch and Trevor strolled back up the road, still playing their imaginary game of football. Jackie sauntered behind them, straining her eyes over her copy of Mr Trim's telegram message.

'Stop!' she suddenly yelled.

The boys spun round.

'Stop!'

'We have stopped, Jackie, or haven't you noticed?' sighed Trevor.

'No, I've found the "stop" word in the telegram. It's "pots", "stop" spelt backwards.'

'What about the other words?' asked Trevor impatiently.

Butch took a dusty stick of chalk from his pocket. 'I knew when I took this from old Mother Henessey's desk that it would come in useful one day. And it has. Definitely!'

He bent down and in large capital letters began to write out the message on the pavement, starting every word with its last letter and ending every word with its first letter.

He got as far as ADDED TO EGGS before Trevor said in a quiet voice, 'I think you should stop now, Butch.'

Butch looked up and nodded.

'I mean,' Trevor went on, 'you never know who might see the message scrawled out on the pavement . . .'

'Yeah, the Birdman,' muttered Butch.

'Or Badger and Miss MacBride,' added Jackie.

Trevor paused. 'Or Mr Trim,' he said, but he didn't dare look Jackie in the eye.

# 6 Proof at last!

They scraped Butch's chalk-writing with their feet, rubbing out all the letters and leaving dusty white circles on the pavement that looked like a small child's picture of clouds.

Jackie started running and the boys followed her. They knew instinctively where she was making for: the ROSIE. They could finish decoding Mr Trim's 'Welsh' telegram there without the danger of being disturbed by the Birdman, or anybody else—except Sharon, of course, who would be busy painting her water-cans anyway.

As they clambered noisily down the narrow steps and into the snug little cabin, Jackie looked around at the familiar furnishings—Sharon's brightly-coloured pots and pans, the tiny frilly curtains, the highly polished wooden table—and she felt suddenly safe and secure. In the world outside, nothing was what it seemed to be; the quest to save the peregrine falcon was like a deadly game where you didn't know whose side anybody was really on.

Sharon's bright and friendly voice called from the galley, 'Tea and buns, you lot?'

All she received by way of an answer were three short grunts from three frowning heads poured over some old bits of paper on the table.

'Kids!' Sharon shook her head.

It did not take Jackie, Trevor and Butch long to work out the rest of the coded message. It stared up at them in Butch's rather wobbly handwriting for them all to see:

ADDED TO EGGS NOW HAVE PEREGRINE FALCON STOP TWO THOUSAND POUNDS STOP WILL BRING BOTH TONIGHT STOP TRIM

It seemed to taunt and mock them as they looked at each other in anger, desperation and despair.

There was no possible doubt now, surely. They had all been taken for fools.

'And we've sent the telegram for them!'

'Actually helped the falcon thieves!' The image of the frightened bird of prey, cowering in Badger's wicker basket, flashed back through Trevor's agonised mind.

'Come on, clear all this stuff off.' Sharon's

voice was bright and business-like. With much nudging and whispering, Jackie and the boys covered the decoded message with their hands. All three of them looked up shiftily at Sharon.

'And what's with all this secrecy and whispering all of a sudden?'

'Er . . . nothing.' Jackie's reply sounded hollow and unconvincing.

'A sweet nothing or a sour nothing?' teased Sharon.

Quickly, as a way of preventing her asking further awkward questions, Jackie turned to help Sharon with the plates and cups on the tray.

'By the way, I saw something in the evening paper that might interest you.' Sharon picked up a newspaper from the window seat and opened it out onto the table. Staring up at them was a photograph of a proud, majestic bird; a bird they now recognised immediately as being a peregrine falcon. 'Is this picture like that bird you saw?'

None of them answered, for they had all turned their eyes to the accompanying headline. FALCON THIEF STRIKES AGAIN! it screamed.

'Well?' Sharon was beginning to find

Jackie and the boys' behaviour distinctly odd and more than a little irritating.

'Might be . . .' shrugged Jackie, absent-mindedly.

Trevor felt some sort of explanation was needed. 'Er . . . well, we didn't see ours properly.'

'Definite—' began Butch, then for once changed his mind. 'No, not really.'

Sharon gave a sigh of despair and went back into the galley. As soon as her back was turned, Jackie, Trevor and Butch craned their necks over the newspaper, rushing through the story that ran under the headline and picture.

# FALCON THIEF STRIKES AGAIN

**ANOTHER peregrine falcon has been stolen from its nest in Scotland. Experts from the Royal Society for the Protection of Birds think the thief was a woman. She may be hiding in London now.**

She always dresses in black. Experts call her Cat Mary because she steals so many birds.

'A woman? Dressed all in black? That *has* to be that creepy Miss MacBride!' exclaimed Jackie.

'Let's tell the fuzz!' suggested Trevor, excitedly.

'Definitely.' For once Butch was in complete agreement with Trevor.

Jackie sat quite still, staring out in front of her, way past the boys. The enormity of the truth had dawned on her, but she couldn't, *wouldn't* believe it. None of this could have anything to do with Mr Trim. He wasn't a ruthless bird thief, he was a friend, one of the few adult friends that Jackie had ever had. She shook her head determinedly. 'No! Mr Trim isn't mixed up in this. He can't be!'

'But it was Trim's telegram!' Trevor yelled impatiently.

'They might have forced him to write it! Hasn't your stupid brain thought of that?' She was clutching at straws now, desperate for any idea that would allow her to believe that Mr Trim wasn't a bird thief after all.

Trevor took a pace back from Jackie. He had never seen such anger in her eyes before. It puzzled, frightened him.

'Yes, well, I suppose that Cat Mary is enough to scare anyone,' conceded Trevor.

'Definitely,' said Butch.

'We'll go and see if Mr Trim has gone back to the shop.' Jackie spoke as if she was giving an order, rather than making a suggestion. The boys scrambled out of their seats to follow her. Butch, in his haste, knocked his cup of tea over the newspaper and telegram message.

'Look what you've done! Clumsy!' chided Trevor. 'Now we can't read the address.' For half a second they thought about trying to clear up the mess, but Jackie was already half way up the steps to the deck.

Sharon was half way down them.

'Where are you off to now?'

'Mr Trim's shop,' blustered Jackie, pushing past her cousin.

Out the corner of her eye, Sharon spotted the overturned teacup. 'Hey! What about helping to clear up this mess . . . it looks like a chimpanzees' tea-party! Honestly!'

Jackie ignored her. 'Won't be long,' she yelled, with no hint of an apology.

Sharon went down into the cabin, picked up the soggy newspaper and tossed it into the bin. Underneath she found the plate of iced buns, untouched and going slowly stale. She sighed. She had bought them as a special treat. Now they would go to waste.

'Kids!' muttered Sharon bitterly. 'I don't understand them. I really don't.'

And with a feeling of sadness and hurt, she stuffed an iced bun into her mouth.

CLOSED said the sign on the door of Mr Trim's shop. The dusty white blind was still down across the front window.

'I knew it!' exclaimed Trevor. 'He's scarpered! We'll have to call the fuzz now!'

'Definitely!'

Jackie turned the door handle. It opened. 'Told you so,' said her look to Trevor.

They closed the door behind them and stood for a moment just inside the shop, letting their eyes grow used to the strange darkness until they could just make out the shapes of the old tables and chests.

'Mr Trim?' called Jackie, hoping against hope to hear a cheery reply of 'Ah, my little sailor friends!' But the only answer was the unhurried ticking of the clocks.

A thin column of dusty light marked a half-open door at the back of the shop.

'Where's that go to?' asked Trevor.

Jackie shrugged. Butch picked his way carefully through the jungle of old furniture and peered gingerly round the door. 'Stairs,' he said. 'Come on, I'm going up.'

The stairs were uncarpeted and with each tread came the sound of a tired creak. When they reached the top, Butch called out, 'Mr Trim?'

No reply.

Just to the left of them stood a grimy door, ajar. Fear does strange things to the mind; to Butch it made him remember his manners. He knocked gingerly on the door and coughed politely.

No reply.

Butch pushed the door open and crept in, followed quickly by Jackie and Trevor.

It was the smell that they noticed first. A sharp, sweet, chemical smell; but coupled with a smell of decay, a smell of death. The glass cabinets that hung from every wall of the room told the story. Although the light from the murky windows was dim, it was bright enough to reveal the contents of the glass cabinets. In every one was a bird. A dead bird. Still, silent and stuffed. Some sat on fake branches, some straddled nests, others had their wings spread in a gruesome mockery of the majesty of flight. There were small birds: finches, tits, a kingfisher; and larger birds: kestrels, hawks and, in a case above the mantlepiece, peregrine falcons.

Butch moved from glass cabinet to glass cabinet, looking away each time his eyes caught the unseeing stare of stuffed creatures.

Jackie seemed quite unable to move. She stood in the centre of the room, just looking,

shaking her head sadly and slowly.

Trevor's attention had been caught by a number of chests with very narrow drawers that lined the walls. He pulled timidly at one of the drawers and it slid easily open. It was full of birds' eggs, all labelled and displayed in neat rows, like items in a jeweller's shop. Curlew, redshank, tree pipit, chiffchaff, wood warbler, yellowhammer . . . the names seemed almost magical and Trevor tried saying them over and over again to himself. But there was no doubt about it, the proper place for these eggs was not a chest of drawers but in a nest, just as the proper place for a bird was not a glass cabinet or a

wicker basket but in the wide blue sky.

Trevor turned on Jackie, unable to hide his anger and disgust. 'What do you make of your friend Trim now? Just a friendly old man, is he?'

'Perhaps he collected these a long time ago when he was young, before peregrine falcons and birds' eggs were protected by law . . .' her voice drifted off; she had not even convinced herself with her explanation of the old man's behaviour, let alone Trevor.

'What a collection! There's eggs in every one of these chests of drawers!' gasped Butch.

'Chest of drawers,' echoed Trevor quietly. '"E.G." Eggs! Remember?'

Butch looked blank, a vague recollection of one of Trevor's awful jokes flitting across his mind.

'On the notice in the shop about that five-hundred-pound chest of drawers in Trim's shop. It said "with contents, e.g."'

'Oh yes! "E.g. rare specimens!" I thought that was one of your so-called jokes.'

'It was! But it was also a code! Come on!'

Butch and Trevor ran back down to the shop, with Jackie, still fearful of the inevitable truth, following.

'They won't budge,' muttered Butch, tugging at the drawers in the £500 chest.

'They wouldn't move when the Birdman tried to open them,' recalled Trevor.

Trevor peered round the side of the chest.

'He's screwed the drawers in!'

Butch took a penknife from his pocket and began to work on the two small screws. They came out easily. Trevor slid the top drawer open. There, wrapped in cotton, was a row of eggs, each one about the size of an ordinary chicken's egg. Trevor picked up a slip of paper that was lying in the drawer.

01 NOCLAF SGGE, it read.

'Ten falcons' eggs. As if we couldn't have guessed!'

'Definitely! Proof at last,' nodded Butch.

Jackie said nothing.

'Yes indeed,' agreed a familiar voice behind them.

Jackie, Butch and Trevor turned round.

'Mr Trim!' whispered Jackie.

The old antique shop owner, the kindly old gentleman they had all trusted as a friend, stood behind them. On either side of him were Cat Mary and Badger. In Badger's hand was the wicker basket, and in the wicker basket was the peregrine falcon.

'Ah, my little sailor friends! Very clever. As you so rightly point out, you have your proof at last!'

Mr Trim had lost his smile completely.

Instead his expression and his words suggested a quiet but chilling menace.

# 7 A friend in need

For a split second, Trevor, Butch and Jackie stood frozen with fear, as silent and as still as the lifeless birds upstairs.

Then Jackie screamed, 'Run for it!' All her feelings of hurt and betrayal vanished as she suddenly realised the danger they were in.

The effect of the sheer terror in Jackie's voice was like that of an electric shock: the boys jolted into life and turned on their heels towards the back door.

'Get them!' Cat Mary yelled at Badger, who dropped the wicker basket and lumbered forward towards Jackie. With strength she never realised she had, Jackie shoved the chest of drawers across the floor, in front of the advancing Badger. She just had time to see his cheeks explode as the corner of the chest caught him a glancing blow in the stomach. Then she too turned and ran for the back door.

'Careful! My eggs! My eggs!' whimpered a distraught Mr Trim, grabbing Badger's collar as he tried to up-end the chest in order to make a way through. Badger pushed Mr Trim back, and the old man tottered and fell to the floor.

'Move yourself, Trim,' shrieked Cat Mary, as she and Badger clambered carelessly over him in their frantic efforts to reach the back door and Jackie.

Mr Trim picked himself up and, wheezing like an old pair of bellows, stumbled after his departing colleagues.

Cat Mary and Badger reached the back yard just in time to see Butch struggling over the wall. Used as he was to running, Butch was not a good climber. Trevor was tall and Jackie was light on her feet; they had both scaled the wall without difficulty. But Butch was heavily built and having problems.

'Help me!' he yelled, and immediately felt his arm being tugged by Trevor on the other side of the wall. He gave one final push with his foot on an old chair they had stood at the base of the wall, and finally he was over—just as he felt Badger's sharp fingernails claw at his ankle.

Badger climbed onto the chair in a desperate effort to pursue Butch, but the seat collapsed under his considerable bulk and the panting bird thief crashed to the yard floor, cursing and swearing.

'Get up, you great whale!' yelled Mr Trim,

as he unlocked the back gate.

'Get after them, you fool!' screamed Cat Mary, her eyes blazing. 'You're meant to be the action man in this outfit!'

Trevor, Butch and Jackie scrambled down the steps that led to the towpath. They were still some way off from the safety of the ROSIE and already they could hear Badger's curses getting nearer and nearer.

Suddenly, on the opposite side of the canal, Jackie spotted a man in a smart blue fisherman's jersey. He was about to open the lock gate to let his boat through.

'Hey!' she called.

Trevor saw the chance too. 'Wait a minute, guv! We'll open the lock for you!' and he and Jackie and Butch raced across the lock to the man in the jersey. His look of sheer amazement suggested that he wasn't used to being hailed as 'guv'. But he had no time to argue with the trio, for already Trevor had grabbed the lock key and was turning the handle of the lock furiously.

Badger thundered onto the lock, but he was too late. The gap was already opening in front of him. He jumped wildly for the far side, missed his footing, then dropped with

a satisfying splash into the canal.

'Thanks, mate,' said Trevor, as he handed the lock key back to the astonished boat owner.

'This way,' called Jackie. 'There's a bridge down there. We can get back on the right side of the canal for the ROSIE!'


Butch was on the bridge, but Trevor was tiring and Jackie could feel the sharp stabbing pain of a stitch in her spine. They stopped to get their breath back, hidden from view by the high sides of the old iron footbridge. None of them had breath left to speak, so that when they looked up and saw Cat Mary and Mr Trim racing up the steps, they just gasped. Then they turned and ran—straight into the waiting arms of a soaking-wet and furious Badger.

'Gotcha!' Badger held the struggling, clawing Jackie fast.

'Leave me!' she screamed to the boys. 'Run for help!'

Avoiding a last minute lunge from Cat Mary and an attempt by Mr Trim to trip them up with his walking stick, Trevor and Butch hurried over the bridge and up the steps at the other side, onto the road. They looked round and saw that Cat Mary and

Mr Trim were already halfway up the steps after them. They ran to the corner and turned into a narrow street. A small van was parked at the kerb, the passenger door open.

'Quick! Jump in!' yelled the driver.

In their desperate bid to escape from Cat Mary and Mr Trim, all the warnings Butch and Trevor had ever had about jumping into strange cars suddenly meant nothing. Startled, but relieved, they tumbled into the passenger seat. The driver leaned over and shut the door. Only then did they look up and see his face. It was a face they recognised as soon as they saw the dark, brooding eyes.

It was the face of the Birdman.

'Get down! And stay down!'

Trevor and Butch obeyed without protest. They were too breathless, too confused to argue. The Birdman threw a blanket over them, while he himself slid down the driver's seat until he was below the level of the windscreen.

'Not a sound!' he whispered.

Trevor and Butch heard footsteps outside the van, and then the angry mutter of voices.

'. . . Just wait till I lay my hands on them children . . .' Cat Mary.

' . . .They can't have gone very far. . .' Mr Trim.

The boys jumped as they heard a thump on the side of the van. Cat Mary's fist.

Eventually the voices drifted off into the distance. Trevor and Butch peeked out from under the blanket and saw the Birdman peering cautiously through the windscreen.

'They've gone.' He pulled the blanket off the two boys, roughly. 'Right, you two.' He sounded as though he meant business. 'Just who are you? And what are you up to?'

Butch did not intend being taken for a fool twice in one day. 'Who are *you*?' he demanded with a purposeful glower.

Trevor picked up the cue. 'Yes! And what are *you* up to?'

For a moment, it looked as if the Birdman was going to lose his temper. Then he shrugged, and gave a sort of half-smile. 'OK, OK. I'm Tom Roberts—from the Royal Society for the Protection of Birds.'

Trevor laughed, cynically. 'We've already had Mr Trim and his English Lovers of the Falcon Society.'

'Lovers of *what* society?' The Birdman fumbled in his pocket and took out his wallet. He flicked it open to reveal an identity card. RSPB, it read. TOM ROBERTS: INVESTIGATIONS OFFICER. There was a signature and a passport photo of the Birdman, and a logo in the corner.

'I've seen that badge on car stickers,' said Trevor. The Birdman nodded. Butch shot a doubtful glance at Trevor.

'OK,' said Trevor, regaining his sense of aggression, 'then what do you *do*?'

Tom Roberts half-smiled again. 'I'm a sort of detective. I've been chasing Cat Mary for weeks.'

'So you didn't steal the falcon, then?'

'I don't steal birds. I protect them!' A look of outrage crossed Tom Robert's face. 'That's why I'm in the RSPB,' he added, crisply.

Trevor nodded. The Birdman might be a

bit gruff but he was straight, and Trevor for one believed him.

Butch nodded. He was beginning to believe the Birdman too.

'Now I think it's about time you told me who *you* are.'

Between them, Trevor and Butch poured out the whole story of Mr Trim and his shop, the chest of drawers and the 'Welsh' telegram.

Tom sat for a moment, drumming his fingers nervously on the steering wheel. 'Hmmmm . . . they'll be on their guard now.' He suddenly stopped. 'I thought there were three of you. Two boys and . . .' He searched Trevor's and Butch's eyes.

Trevor and Butch nodded glumly.

' . . . What's happened to the girl?'


'Put her in the corner, Badger!' rasped Cat Mary. 'And you,' she stabbed her piercing eyes in Jackie's direction, 'don't you move!'

They were back at the shop. Mr Trim was busily collecting the eggs from the chest of drawers. Cat Mary went over to the wicker basket, then stopped in her tracks. The catch holding the lid was broken. There was no sign of the falcon.

'Badger!' she screamed. 'Where's the falcon?'

Badger stared in anguish at the wicker basket.

'When you went after those kids, you dropped the basket . . . !'

'You told me to chase them.'

'You fool!' Badger stepped back as Mr Trim waved his stick at him. 'You've just lost us two thousand pounds!'

'It's always my fault . . . I said to keep the kids out of it . . .'

'Stop blubbering, man!'

Cat Mary snapped her fingers. Mr Trim and Badger looked up.

'There's just one place in London where we can find another one.'

'Another peregrine falcon? Impossible!'

But Cat Mary wasn't listening to Mr Trim. 'Badger, keep hold of the girl. We must get out of here and hide somewhere until it's dark.'

'What about the girl?' asked Mr Trim.

'Huh! She's *your* problem.'

'I know somewhere, up by the canal at Maida Vale. There's a shed by the tunnel.'

'Right! We'll dump you two there first. Let's move!' Cat Mary barked out her order.

Badger grabbed Jackie's arm, and her hand skidded across a dusty mirror.

'Don't hurt her,' said Mr Trim, with real authority in his voice. But he could not bring himself to look Jackie in the face, nor did she want him to.

Cat Mary was not concerned with Jackie. 'Lead the way, Trim,' she snapped. 'And don't worry, your buyer will have his peregrine falcon by . . .' She looked at her watch. 'Shall we say . . . midnight?'

## 8   Where is Jackie?

The Birdman sat hunched over the steering wheel, concentrating on his driving. He looked anxious and tense.

But he said nothing.

Trevor sat glumly in the back of the old van. All day he had been willing there to be some *action*. But now there was some, he wasn't enjoying it very much. He kept thinking about Jackie. He wished he had ignored her advice now and stayed on the bridge to fight Badger and Cat Mary.

But he said nothing.

Butch wondered what Sharon would say, when she found out that they had let Jackie be kidnapped. It would mean trouble, he was sure of that. Memories of the telling-offs he had received from his mum whenever he had let one of his little sisters get dirty or cross the road without looking came flooding back.

But he said nothing.

The old van spluttered and rattled its way along the busy London streets. Taxis, delivery vans, even buses overtook them.

Just as on their last visit, the boys tiptoed into Mr Trim's shop and found it empty. This time, though, it was even quieter. It was Mr Trim's habit to wind his clocks up at midday everyday. Today, of course, he had been otherwise engaged and some of the clocks had already stopped ticking.

'You say you're staying with Jackie's cousin?' asked the Birdman, suddenly.

Trevor noticed that the Birdman spoke a bit like Sharon did. Instead of saying 'cousin', he said it more like 'cossun'.

'We'd better let her know what's happened,' said the Birdman.

'We can get hold of her at the craft shop. Definitely,' said Butch. 'I'll phone her, if you like.'

The Birdman looked relieved. 'Right. Yes . . .'

As Butch leant against the wall, telephone in hand, Trevor thought how strangely grown up he looked. He spoke clearly and calmly to Sharon, telling her not to worry. When he put the phone down, he said, 'She's coming right over.'

'If only we could've got here a few minutes earlier.' The Birdman sounded desperate.

To try and ease the situation, Butch said,

'I lost my little sister once, in Woolworth's.'
And then wished he hadn't.

'Jackie's not *lost*,' snapped the Birdman,
'and she's not with a bunch of friendly shop
assistants either.'

There was a long silence. Nobody seemed
to know quite what to do.

'Let's try and think where they might have
taken her.'

'That old house by the canal?'

The Birdman shook his head. 'Too
dangerous for them by half.'

'Hey, look at this!' Trevor beckoned Butch
and the Birdman over to where he was
standing by an old mirror in the corner of
the shop. 'There's some writing on this—in
the dust—see?'

'Looks like a lot of names . . . Alma, Ida, Val. Girls' names. Some lad with a lot of girlfriends, I expect.'

The shop bell tinkled furiously and Sharon burst in.

'I ran all the way,' she spluttered breathlessly. 'Any news?'

All three shook their heads.

'I'm sorry, Sharon . . .' began Butch, but she ignored him.

'Have you phoned the police?'

All three shook their heads.

'I've got a contact in the CID who's involved in the Cat Mary affair,' said the Birdman.

'Right. You'd better ring him. And I'd better ring Jackie's mum,' said Sharon.

'By the way, Sharon,' said Trevor. 'This is the Birdman . . . er . . . Mr Roberts . . . er . . . Tom. He's a bird detective with the RSPB.'

Sharon nodded to Tom, briefly.

'And this is Sharon, Jackie's cousin,' added Trevor.

Tom managed a worried kind of smile.

'He talks just like you do,' whispered Trevor to Sharon.

While Tom and Sharon busied themselves on the telephone, Trevor and Butch studied the writing on the mirror.

'I'm sure it's from Jackie,' said Trevor.

'It could be in code! Definitely. She's used a code! Just like Trim. Spell it backwards.'

'She wouldn't use Trim's code—not if he was with her. Use your brain, Butch.'

But Butch was too busy working the code out to be bothered by Trevor's taunts. 'I am, dumbo. Look.'

Butch put his hand over the 'MA' of ALMA. 'Read to me, Trevor.'

'What is this? Jackanory?' But Trevor began reading. 'CAN . . . AL. Canal!'

'Now this.' Butch put his hand over the 'AL' of ALMA.

'Maida! Jackie's code was to put the gaps between the words in the wrong place!'

'CANAL MAIDA VALE TUN!' announced Butch triumphantly.

'Maida Vale is just up the canal!'

'But what does TUN mean?'

Trevor shrugged. Butch shook his head sadly. Then they stared hard at each other.

'Trev . . . ?'

'Butch?'

'You know who's fault it is that Jackie's in this mess?'

Trevor nodded. 'Ours.'

They glanced across the shop to where Tom was still deep in conversation on the phone, watched intently by Sharon.

'Then I reckon it's up to us to find her. Come on.'

Dodging behind chests and bookcases, Trevor and Butch slipped out of the shop without Sharon or Tom noticing, and headed straight for the canal at Maida Vale.

On the far side of the canal, four tall blocks of grey flats loomed out of the gathering dusk. Every now and then, a light would go on in one of the windows. It was getting late. Butch and Trevor paused for breath on the towpath.

'Tun, tun, tun,' Butch kept saying to himself again and again. 'Perhaps it's part of the name of a boat.'

With a sigh, they gazed out at the rows of boats bobbing gently up and down on the canal. They looked at a few names: Silver Crest, Prince Regent, Quiet Days.

'I can't imagine Cat Mary having a boat called Quiet Days, can you?' snorted Butch. But Trevor was beyond laughing at Butch's feeble jokes.

'It could be any one of these. There's hundreds!'

'There's even more through the other side of the tunnel,' sighed Butch.

'Through the what?' Trevor had suddenly stopped reading the names of the boats and was looking hard at Butch.

'That tunnel—over the canal.'

'That's it! Tun, tun, tunnel! That's what Jackie was going to write, when she was stopped.'

Inside the tunnel, the air smelt damp and chilly. The sound of the boys' footsteps rang noisily around the steeply curved walls with a dull echo. As they approached the far end, they could see a figure sitting hunched on a stool in front of an old shed. Although the figure had his back to them, Butch and Trevor recognised the long silver hair and the knobbly walking stick immediately.

'Trim!'

'Let's get him!' Trevor's thirst for action was overwhelming.

'Hang on,' said Butch cautiously, 'we don't know who might be around with him. No, let's make him come into the tunnel.'

Butch gathered up a handful of pebbles

and tossed them into the canal. They made a satisfying splash, but Mr Trim didn't move an inch. Butch clapped his hands loudly, so that the sound echoed around the tunnel walls like rifle fire. Mr Trim still didn't move.

'It's no good,' sighed Butch. 'The old beggar's as deaf as a post.'

'Tell you what,' whispered Trevor, 'if I go and distract him, he'll chase me back into the tunnel, won't he?'

'Worth a try. Definitely,' said Butch, but he didn't sound convinced.

Trevor was already off, though. He strode right up behind Mr Trim and coughed loudly. As the old man turned round in amazement, Trevor leapt back and dashed for the safety of the tunnel. Mr Trim staggered up and tottered after him. Butch tried his famous flying rugby tackle, but Mr Trim, stronger, fitter and more determined than they had ever imagined, shook him off. He made for Trevor, who picked up a lifebelt from the side of the tunnel and, lifting it high above his head, brought it down in one fast movement over the old man's shoulders.

'Gotcha! as Badger would say,' yelled Trevor. 'Now tell us where Jackie is.'

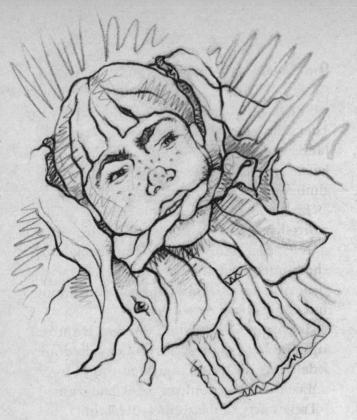

The old man kicked and groaned. Then the boys heard a thumping sound coming from an old boathouse by the tunnel entrance. While Butch held the lifebelt fast round Mr Trim's shoulder's, Trevor ran across to the shed and pulled a long iron bar from the door.

There, hardly visible in the late evening gloom but staring up at them in anger and fear, was the bound and gagged figure of Jackie.

## 9 Trim's trick

They used the ropes and rags that had held Jackie to tie Mr Trim's wrists and ankles. Jackie and the boys were giggling, laughing, almost crying with relief and excitement.

'Bet you were scared,' said Trevor, with more than a hint of admiration in his voice.

'No,' shrugged Jackie, unconvincingly. The boys looked at her suspiciously. 'I mean,' Jackie went on, 'I *knew* you would find me.'

'Simple, really,' said Butch, with a kind of superior air, 'just a matter of cracking your code.'

'Eventually,' added Jackie with a grin.

Trevor was dancing up and down, excitedly. 'We'll get the fuzz here, and then when Cat Mary and Badger come back for him,' he jerked a thumb in Mr Trim's direction, 'we'll nab them! See!'

'Action man has spoken,' groaned Butch.

'Watch it,' said Trevor.

'I only . . .'

'Stop it, you two! Why are you always arguing?'

'Because we're mates,' explained Trevor.

Jackie shook her head in despair. 'Look.

Cat Mary and Badger aren't coming back here. Badger lost the falcon—'

'Again?' asked Trevor, incredulously.

'Again,' said Jackie, 'and they're going to get another one from somewhere, then they're going straight onto the French boat.'

'What, the one we sent the "Welsh" telegram to? *His* rich customer?' Trevor jerked his thumb at Mr Trim again. Jackie nodded. Then her anger finally broke through.

'You . . . you should be ashamed of yourself, Mr Trim!' She stared him hard in the face.

'Should I? Why?' Mr Trim wriggled around, straining the knots on the ropes round his wrists and ankles. He sounded defiant, sulky, like a small child who knows he has done wrong but won't admit it.

'Because you only *pretend* to love falcons!'

'I *do* love falcons!' It was Mr Trim's turn to become angry.

'But you *kill* them! And steal their eggs! You call that love?'

'I am a collector.' Mr Trim was growing ever-so-slightly flustered. 'And . . . and collecting eggs, er . . . helps one study—'

But the hurt that Jackie had felt at Mr Trim's betrayal was driving her on. 'Every egg you collect means one more dead falcon! Why do you need so many eggs? Why?'

'Because . . . because . . .'

Actually, Jackie knew why. Trevor and Butch knew why. But they wanted to hear it from Mr Trim's own lips.

'Go on! Because what?' Butch and Trevor shrank back from the fierceness of Jackie's fury.

'Because . . . because the more one has, well, the more valuable—'

'Ah! That's it, isn't it?' shouted Jackie triumphantly. Her eyes blazed down into Mr Trim's ashen face. They seemed at that moment, to Mr Trim, to carry more threat and more danger than even Cat Mary's eyes. 'Money! You don't really want to protect wild birds. You only like them when they're dead and stuffed and standing about in your grisly collection! All *you* want is *money*!'

'And you said so yourself, if things go on as they are, there will be no more falcons!' Trevor was keen to have his say.

'Yes! People like you and Cat Mary, with your stealing and selling, you're putting an end to them all!' Butch wasn't going to be left out.

'I hope . . . I hope . . .' Trevor thought of

all the nasty things he hoped would happen to Mr Trim. 'I hope they put you in prison! In a cage!'

'Yes. Definitely. Just like you've been trying to put that poor falcon in a cage!'

Jackie turned away. She was close to tears. 'I still can't believe that someone we liked, who seemed so nice, could turn out to be so rotten . . . underneath . . .' She stopped. She had finally run out of anger and words.

Butch went and put an arm round Jackie's shoulder, the way he did to his younger sister if their dad had shouted at her. 'He's not worth it, Jackie,' he said quietly. 'Come on, let's call the police and get it over with.'

'Wait!' whispered Mr Trim, anxiously.

'Wait for what?' Butch's tone was as sharp as a knife.

For the first time since he had revealed himself to be in league with Cat Mary, Mr Trim found the courage to face Jackie. 'You know I never meant you any harm, Jackie, my dear . . .'

'No harm? You shut her in that old shed!'

Mr Trim bowed his head, thoughtfully, as if he was trying to find an answer to Butch's accusation. Then he said quietly, 'I'm sorry.'

'It's easy to say that now,' answered Butch harshly.

Mr Trim looked up. He took a deep breath. 'Cat Mary and Badger *are* going to steal another peregrine falcon—from the zoo,' he said.

Trevor and Butch studied Mr Trim's gaunt features. Was this a trap?

'They're going to climb in from the canal path—with a rope-ladder. Just as soon as it gets dark.'

'It's almost dark now,' said Butch, looking around at the lengthening shadows in alarm.

Then Jackie spoke, her voice even and calm now. 'Will you help us, Mr Trim?'

Butch and Trevor shot each other anxious glances.

'If you will trust me,' replied Mr Trim, hesitantly.

'It may be a trap,' said Trevor. He and Butch looked to Jackie for some guidance. Once more, she seemed to have the authority.

'I trust him,' she said, quietly.

Butch shrugged, then nodded.

Trevor said nothing. He began easing the rope from Mr Trim's wrists and Jackie started to untie the knots round his ankles.

'Come on, you big baby!' Cat Mary peered down from the top of the wall that ran round the perimeter of the zoo. At the bottom of the wall stood Badger, staring at a rope-ladder that was swinging gently in the late evening breeze.

'It keeps wobbling!' Badger put one foot on the bottom rung and grasped the ladder desperately, like a storm-tossed sailor clinging to the mast.

'Keep your eyes closed, then!'

Cat Mary looked at her watch. The luminous dial showed nine o'clock. They had to find the bird house, get the falcon, get out of the zoo and get to the boat by midnight. They were cutting it fine. But at least Badger seemed to have got the hang of the rope-ladder now.

'Yes . . . it's dead easy with your eyes closed . . .'

Cat Mary glanced down, and then cursed in disbelief as she saw Badger thrash out with his hand for the next rung, miss, overbalance, then topple backwards into the canal.


Badger scrambled onto the towpath and writhed around like a beached whale, splashing water everywhere.

'You'll have to manage without me. I'm a sick man.'

Cat Mary shook her head. 'Get on with it, you great blubbering mass.'

'But . . .'

'Don't worry. I'll be right behind you. With this.' The blade of Cat Mary's sheath-knife flashed menacingly in the moonlight.

Up the rope-ladder went Badger.

A few minutes later, Mr Trim, Jackie and the boys arrived.

'This is their ladder all right,' muttered Mr Trim. 'And judging by its wetness, we're not far behind them.'

'It's all wet here as well,' whispered Trevor, pointing to a pool of water at the foot of the wall. 'It must be Badger. He's fallen in again!'

Jackie and Butch joined in the laughter.

'Quiet!' ordered Mr Trim.

'Will you be OK on the ladder, Mr Trim?' Trevor looked at the frail figure of Mr Trim, doubtfully.

'Listen. I've shinned up more rope-ladders than you've had fish and chip suppers, but we won't go into that now. If you can just throw my stick over . . .'

It was rather like being in the jungle, Trevor thought, as the cries of strange birds and animals broke through the continuous background hum of London traffic. The thick undergrowth was growing wet with dew, and a peculiar smell of wild animals hung on the night air.

They soon found the main path.

'There's a signpost,' whispered Jackie.

110

'Elephants that way, reptiles over there—
birds of prey! That's where they will have
gone!'

'Keep to the shadows,' warned Mr Trim,
'and remember, when we find them, we
must get help. Cat Mary is very dangerous.'

The hair on Jackie's scalp tingled as a
monkey leapt out from behind a rock and
rattled the bars of its cage. She uttered a tiny
cry of shock.

'What's that?' Trevor was alert.

'Me, you idiot,' whispered Jackie.

'No! That squelching sound—'

Too late.

Round the side of the monkey house
came Cat Mary and Badger.

Both groups froze. Then Cat Mary stepped forward, her sheath-knife flashing in her hand.

'What's the big idea, Trim? We're supposed to meet at your customer's boat.' She looked Jackie, Trevor and Butch up and down, as if she wished she could grind them into the ground with her heel. 'And what are those kids doing here?'

Mr Trim laughed. His voice was thin and chill. 'Ah, don't worry. You see they captured me, I'm afraid. Stupid of me, of course. The only way out was to pretend to *join* them.'

The boys turned in horror to Jackie.

'So, I *tricked* them into coming here!'

He spun round and gave the three young friends an icy stare, while behind them the inhabitants of the monkey house tugged at the wire mesh bars of their cages and screeched and hooted at them.

It seemed to Jackie as if the monkeys were laughing wildly at them, mocking them all.

## 10 Back to the wild

'Mr Trim! We trusted you!' Jackie was close to tears. The nightmare was beginning all over again.

'Ah, but you see, my dear little sailor friends, I've tricked you, haven't I?' Mr Trim leered at Jackie. He started to move closer to Cat Mary. 'Oh yes, you have to be very clever to catch an old fox like me.'

Suddenly Mr Trim lunged forward and grabbed Cat Mary's wrist. 'Got you!' he hissed. Cat Mary's face showed no trace of emotion as she brought up the sheath-knife and plunged it into Mr Trim's arm. He reeled back with a cry of pain and then fell heavily to the ground. For a moment, the monkeys stopped their screeching. Then, seeming to sense the fear and danger, they began to leap around their cages, screaming in great high-pitched wails as if they, and not old Mr Trim, had felt the sharp blade of Cat Mary's knife.

'Keep back, Trim, unless you want a cut on the other arm to match!' Cat Mary's eyes were as cold as steel.

Already Jackie had run across to where Mr Trim was lying. She seemed completely unaware of the danger posed by Cat Mary and the gleaming, blood-stained knife.

'Butch! Have you got a hanky?'

Butch started, shocked once again by how easily Jackie seemed able to take control of things. He put his hand in his pocket in a futile gesture and shook his head; he had no use for anything so fancy as a hanky.

'I'm sorry, Jackie. I did try,' mumbled Mr Trim. In the shadowy moonlight his gaunt features were paler than usual.

Sheepishly, Trevor held out a bright white handkerchief to Jackie. It was carefully folded and pressed. Jackie took it and noticed in the corner a scrolled letter T.

'It's my gran. She gives them to me every Christmas. And birthday. And my mum packed me a clean one for every day of the holiday.' Trevor shrugged. As Butch might have said, action man had spoken.

Cat Mary stood a little way off, whispering intently to Badger. 'That stupid girl won't leave Trim. So, you grab the kid in the plaid jacket and I'll grab the other one.'

'Like this you mean?' called a voice behind them. But before Cat Mary had time to turn round, a strong arm held her neck in a vice-like grip and a hand knocked the sheath-knife from her grasp.

Cat Mary tried to yell, but all that came out of her mouth was a watery gurgle. 'Oh no, Cat Mary,' said the voice, 'your "grabbing" days are well and truly over.'

'Tom!' Trevor's eyes strained through the darkness to make out what was going on.

'Grab the big fellow!' yelled Tom. Two burly policemen crashed through the undergrowth. Badger, who had been staring open-mouthed in horror at recent events, dropped the wicker basket and ran for all he was worth.

The policemen leapt over the basket, as if they were more than used to running obstacle races, and set off in pursuit. But

Badger was not a natural athlete and he, as much as anyone, knew it. In a last desperate move, he turned off the gravel path, scrambled over a fence, then came to a small wall. He was about to leap over it when a notice caught his eye. THE SEA LION POOL, it read.

'OK,' groaned Badger despairingly. 'I give up. I've had it up to here with getting wet.' And he meekly held out his arms for the policeman's handcuffs.

At the back of the pool a sea lion lumbered up onto a rock to get a better view of the proceedings and then slid down into the pool, splashing around furiously, as if to show Badger that getting wet could be quite good fun, really.

Jackie stared at Tom in sheer disbelief. 'It's him,' she whispered to Trevor. 'The *Birdman*!'

'That's right,' said Trevor. 'His name's Tom and he's a sort of bird detective really from the Royal Society for the Protection of Birds.'

'You never told me!' Jackie looked quite put out.

'Didn't have time, did we.'

Two more policemen were taking Cat Mary from Tom. 'Trim!' she screamed, her eyes flashing with anger and contempt. 'You're a fool! A bumbling, useless old fool!' Then she was gone, hauled off into the darkness towards an awaiting police car by the two silent constables.

'She's quite right, my dears, of course.' Mr Trim shook his head sadly, then winced as he tried to move his injured arm.

'Don't worry, Mr Trim. They'll get you to hospital, soon.'

'Jackie!' Running along the path came Sharon.

'Sharon?' Jackie turned to the boys. 'Did you tell her?' she asked accusingly.

'Of course we did. We *had* to,' said Butch.

Sharon hugged Jackie, tears streaming down her face. 'Kids,' she mumbled, as laughter mingled with her tears. 'Blooming kids.' Much to their embarrassment, she then turned and hugged first Trevor, then Butch. 'What a crew!' she said.

'They've done well.' Tom came over to join them. 'Very well.' He bent down to look at Mr Trim's injured arm. 'The police will take you to the hospital first, Mr Trim.'

'This is Mr Trim,' said Jackie to Sharon.

'So I guessed,' replied Sharon.

'And this is my cousin Sharon,' said Jackie to Mr Trim.

Mr Trim looked away.

Suddenly Jackie frowned. 'How did you manage to get here, Sharon?'

Sharon grinned. 'In Tom's van, of course.'

'Do you know him, then?'

'Of course she does,' said Trevor. 'And they both talk funny. Just like they do in *Coronation Street*.'

Sharon grinned at Tom.

And he grinned back.


'Come along, Trim. The sooner we get you to hospital, the sooner that arm of yours can be looked at properly.'

'Of course, sergeant.'

'Mr Trim!' Jackie called after the old man and the sergeant as they began to move off. She ran up to them, then not quite knowing what to say, simply mumbled, 'Thank you.'

'Not at all. Thank *you*.'

'Come along, Trim, we haven't got all night,' interrupted the sergeant, impatiently.

'Thank you, all three of you, my little sailor friends.' Mr Trim turned and walked off into the night with the sergeant.

'We'll see you again . . . ?' Jackie's voice

trailed off. Mr Trim and the sergeant were already no more than faint shadows disappearing into the distance.

Jackie rejoined Sharon, Tom and the boys. Sharon put an arm around her shoulders as the group walked slowly back towards the zoo gates.

'How could he have been so deceitful?' asked Jackie, tearfully. 'We were meant to be his friends. We trusted him.' For a moment, nobody, not even Sharon or Tom, seemed to have an answer.

Then suddenly Butch said, 'Like my Uncle Barry. When he came out of the merchant navy, he had pots of money. I went down the market with him and there was this geezer selling bikes, and my Uncle Barry said he would buy me one for Christmas.' Butch paused, as the painful memory came flooding back. 'He never did, though. I spent weeks planning where I was going to go on that bike, but he never bought it for me. He spent all his money buying a rusty old Escort. I hated him for months. He wasn't *bad*, though, just . . .' He searched for the right word.

'Mean?' suggested Trevor.

Butch shook his head. 'Thoughtless.'

'And it *hurt*,' said Sharon.

'Yes,' nodded Butch, thinking of his Uncle Barry's broken promise.

'Yes,' nodded Jackie, thinking of Mr Trim's deceit.

'Sometimes, something sort of drives people to do things completely out of character,' said Tom. 'Mr Trim was driven by love of money. But when you think about it, you lot were driven to do some pretty strange things too.'

Jackie and the boys looked at Tom in puzzlement.

He grinned. 'Look how you lads leapt into my old van. I was a complete stranger. But you were driven by *fear*. Fear of being caught by Cat Mary made *you* act completely out of character. And when you rushed out to find Jackie without telling Sharon or me. That was out of character, but you felt so bad and guilty about having left Jackie to the mercy of Badger that you were driven to do it.'

Trevor and Butch nodded.

'Mind you, that was sharp work working out Jackie's code.'

'Just took a bit of brains, you know,' said Butch airily.

'But how did *you* manage to find us?' enquired a puzzled Trevor.

'I like that!' laughed Tom. 'You're not the

only ones with brains around here. I worked out Jackie's code too—'

'With a bit of help,' Sharon grinned.

'Yes, well . . .' Tom looked a bit embarrassed. 'Then when we told the police, they said they'd had a 999 call from someone who'd seen a gang of hooligans breaking into the zoo.'

'Badger and Cat Mary, you mean,' said Butch.

'No, you three and Mr Trim!' This time it was Sharon's turn to laugh.

When they reached Tom's van, a policeman was waiting for them. 'Just had a radio call,' he said. 'Something about a falcon flying around Trafalgar Square. Anything to do with you?'

'Our falcon!' cried Jackie.

'I'd better get down there quickly,' said Tom, 'before it eats all the pigeons!'


A few days later, Trevor, Butch and Jackie were sitting on the side of the ROSIE, dangling their fishing rods hopefully into the canal.

'They do say there's plenty of kippers in there, somewhere,' chuckled a voice behind them. It was Tom.

'What's the news?' asked Butch.

'I've just come from seeing Mr Trim. His arm's much better. I don't know what you kids did or said to him, but he wants to join the RSPB. He says he's going to fight for the falcon from now on.' Tom paused, thoughtfully. 'What's more, I think he means it.'

Jackie looked long and hard at Tom. 'What's going to *happen* to him?'

'Well, because of his change of heart, and because he tried to help you in the end, he might not go to prison for *so* long.'

'I'll be able to write to him, won't I?'

Tom nodded. 'And I've got something for you! As a reward for all your help, we're making you members of the Young Ornithologists' Club.'

'Orni-what?' asked Butch.

'Ornithologists,' said Tom. 'People who study birds and want to protect them. That's what you three are, after all. You helped to save a wild falcon.'

'What's happened to our falcon?' asked Jackie.

'It's gone to Wales, with a real falconer,' explained Tom.

'Any chance of seeing it?' asked Trevor.

'Well,' Tom hesitated, 'we could do the

trip in a day, I suppose . . .'

Sharon poked her head out of the hatch.
'I thought I heard a familiar voice,' she said,
smiling.

She was met with a chorus of queries:

'Can we go to Wales . . . ?'

'To see the falcon . . . ?'

'Go on, Sharon . . . !'

Sharon glanced at Tom and smiled. 'I
don't see why not.'

'You'll come with us?'

'Love to,' said Sharon.

'Great!' said Trevor.

'Definitely,' echoed Butch.


Over the tree-tops swooped the peregrine
falcon. Then it climbed steeply, high up
towards the afternoon sun.

'Isn't it beautiful, Sharon? Wasn't it worth
all the trouble to try to save it?'

'Oh yes,' said Sharon, not taking her eyes
off it for a moment. 'Oh yes.'

For a few seconds, the falcon hovered
above them, its wings beating the air
furiously.

Click, went Butch's camera. 'Got a great
picture. Definitely!' said Butch, tapping the
50p camera that he had bought from

Mr Trim, the day their hunt for the falcon had begun.

The falconer stood a little apart from Tom, Sharon, Jackie and the boys. Above his head he swung a long rope, on the end of which was a piece of meat disguised to look like a pigeon.

The falcon dived in a deep arc to pluck the meat from the end of the rope.

'He's teaching it to hunt for its own prey, so that it can look after itself,' explained Tom.

'Then it will be a real wild bird again,' said Trevor.

'Yes, a real sky hunter,' murmured Jackie.


Two weeks later, Jackie, Butch and Trevor were lying on the deck of the ROSIE, watching a family of rooks gathering in the trees, when Sharon came in with the post.

'A postcard for you,' she said. 'Guess who from?'

'Tom?'

Sharon nodded and went to the galley door.

'Don't you want to read it too?' asked Jackie.

But Sharon just waved her hand; in it she held the pages of what looked like a very long letter. 'Guess who from?' she giggled, and she gave Jackie a big wink.

'Ah,' grinned Jackie.

Trevor and Butch looked baffled.

'Has Tom written Sharon a letter?' asked Butch.

'Of course!' laughed Jackie.

Trevor frowned. 'What for?' he asked, innocently.

'Sometimes you two are so *thick*,' sighed Jackie.

What Tom said in his postcard to Jackie, Butch and Trevor was:

# Dear Young Ornithologists

Today our peregrine falcon didn't come back to its shed. We watched it hunt its own prey. It doesn't need us any more. We saw it fly away to the mountains. The peregrine has gone back to the wild.

love from
'The Birdman'

But what Tom said in his letter to Sharon, only he and Sharon know.

. . . The driver of the brightly-coloured Birdbus trains her binoculars on the peregrine falcon as it swoops low over the wooded hillside below Yat Rock.

'I wonder what did happen to our peregrine?' she asks her two companions.

'Perhaps that bird up there is a distant relation of our one, eh, Trev?' says the shorter of the two men.

Trevor agrees. 'Could well be, Butch. After all, Wales is only over those hills.'

Butch nods. 'Definitely.' He sighs and looks at his watch. 'Time for us to be getting back to the big city, Jackie.'

The driver of the Birdbus groans. 'Motorways, traffic jams, petrol fumes . . .'

'And work,' adds Trevor, glumly. 'It's back to the office tomorrow.'

'I felt just like this on the last day of that holiday we had on the ROSIE, when I suddenly realised we had to go back to school. I wanted to be a full-time Young Ornithologist!'

'And now you want to be a full-time Birdbus driver?'

Jackie grins. 'Something like that!'

They stood for a moment in silence, transfixed by the sight of the peregrine falcons wheeling high above their heads.

'That holiday on the ROSIE was something *special*, wasn't it?' says Jackie suddenly.

'Of course it was! We didn't know anything about birds before then,' says Butch.

'Speak for yourself,' grins Trevor.

'It was certainly special for Tom and Sharon,' Butch laughs. 'If it hadn't been for us having that holiday, they would never have met and got married.'

'I was thinking more of old Mr Trim,' says Jackie, quietly.

'What a mixed-up geezer,' mutters Butch.

Trevor turns to Jackie. 'Do you still see anything of him?'

'Yes. He's in an old people's home now.'

'Old Mr Trim is?'

'He's *very* old Mr Trim now. You know, there was never a time—not even when I was locked up—when I didn't like him. I think that's why it hurt so much.'

She smiles.

'He's more bird-mad now than the rest of us put together! His room overlooks a big garden, you know. Tom and Sharon bought him some binoculars and he spends all day watching the thrushes, blackbirds, finches . . . He knows all their nesting habits.'

Jackie, Butch and Trevor stroll back to the Birdbus. Jackie starts the engine and swings the bus round onto the narrow dusty lane.

Behind them, the peregrine falcons hover and then swoop down as fast as lightning in great, long curves over the dark tree-tops. *They* are not going back to the town. They are staying here on the thickly wooded cliffs high above Symonds Yat, where there is air and freedom and food in abundance.

It is a good place for a sky hunter.

128